Closed Circle Open World

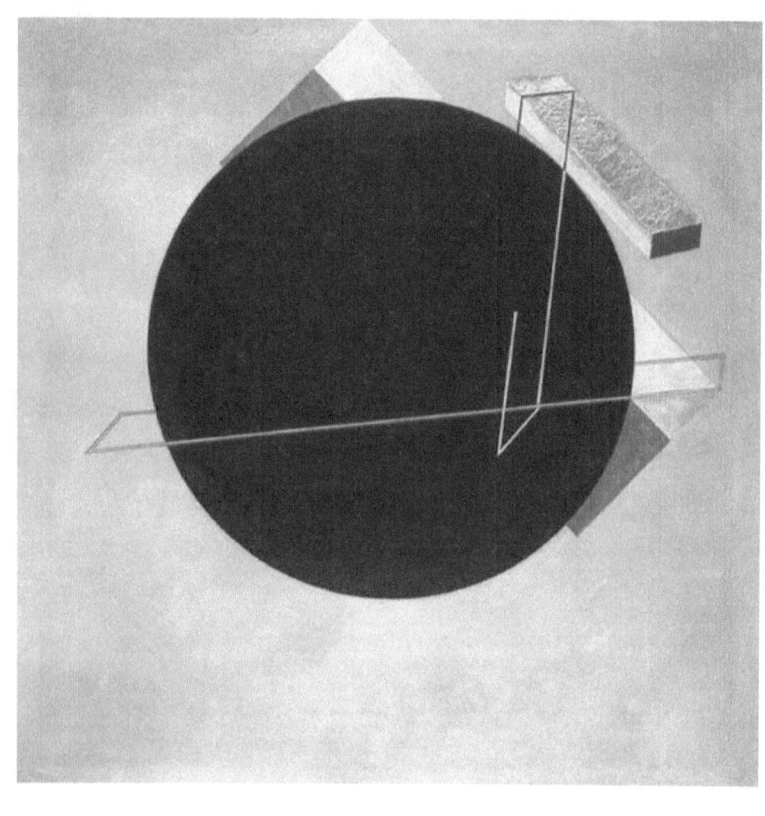

CLOSED CIRCLE

OPEN WORLD

By Shyam Gohel

ISBN 979-8-9985022-7-9

Contents

Place, Time, Characters

Morristown, New Jersey.   April 2, 2126

Zalia   Scientist, dancer

Believes in Reason

"Reason is forever without Ground. Reason leaps ahead. Reason takes risks."

Lina   27 years old, mother of Nanu, musician

Believes in Nature (wildlife) and childhood (play)

"It is culture that allows us to enjoy nature — not the other way around."

Hirshi   10 years old, friend of Nanu

Believes in ambiguity, suffers from anxiety

"The time ahead will be difficult – there is no easy way out, no easy solution."

A2B   Robot

Believes in Language (poetry), lives in pain

$" \phi = 1 + \frac{1}{\phi} "$

Nanu   8 years old, daughter of Lina, friend of Hirshi

Believes in calmness (letting things be, an attitude of relaxed freedom)

". . . (listen to A2B), and change your life."

". . . each of us has faith, but everything depends on how we believe in our faith."

Walter Benjamin   (1892 – 1940)

Chapter One

This Dance (Zinzoti)

The mathematics are not important.

Two numbers are important: 61 and 601.

Five names are important: Zalia, Lina, Hirshi, A2B, and Nanu.

Date: 2

Month: April

Year: 2126

There's a y-Normid meteor shower — in the constellation Norma, above the horizon, at radiant points — in the sky.

Bats, owls, night herons, endangered pangolins, stray and feral cats wake up later than usual, because the new moon from nine nights ago is still in the sky.

Day and night are truly opposites these days.

People make wishes during the day, then wait for their wishes to come true at night.

But night does not *become* day, these days.

Night *gives way* to day, the way primary colors *give way* to softer, secondary colors.

Night and day are made of the same stuff — time — but the two are as far apart as night and day.

Cold wave conditions have continued on through the nights for the last four months.

A fresh spell of dense to very dense fog has been predicted for tonight but hasn't happened yet.

Nothing that has been predicted in the last 100 years has come true.

There're the sounds of the seas from miles and miles away — up to 34 miles away — creating a wishing-washing-gushing movement, followed by a hollow-legato-swallowing buffalo-sized silence.

The sounds of these waters at a distance keep most people calm and able to sleep at night.

So long as there is plenty of water, there is life.

So long.

As there is.

Water.

So long.

Life.

So long.

Life, up to this day 2126, has been the mirror of nature: ebb and flow, wax and wane, agonism and antagonism, arrogant rise and tragic fall (or, the other way around: first the fall, then redemption), arrival and departure.

Sounds of water growing louder and louder have signaled to most people that the world is *not at all* ending.

The world is *not ending*.

But, sometimes, the coming of something new — like a close encounter, or, an encounter of the first kind (whereby something, which leaves no evidence of its presence, is merely noticed) — is very, very daunting.

61, 601, Zalia, Lina, Hirshi, A2B, Nanu, 2 April 2126, astronomical, lunar, nautical, wildlife disturbances abound: our story has begun, "Closed Circle Open World."

Closed circle.

Open world.

Even while the whole world changes, you may choose not to change.

But stories — like the present one, dear reader — are never told about the people who choose to stay the same.

If you make it to the end of this story and decide that *you would absolutely be one of us who would consider change*, then why wouldn't you do it this very day?

Why not this very day?

Change.

Why not?

This very day.

Why not.

No matter whatever else is going on in the world, *you,* in your buzzing mind, with your unknown emotions, as if seas were overflowing and emptying inside of you — gushing and parting inside of you — *have the power to make your life.*

Take steps.

What will you eat?

What will you swallow?

What will you believe?

What will you fall for?

The mood is set.

Let us come down to the personal level.

This story is about when great disturbances become very fine, very private, very ticklish revolutions.

No one can opt out of a revolution.

From now on, everyone will be moving either

backward, starboard, toppled, wandered, or awkward.

This new Order of Life on Earth, beginning 2 April 2126, is called Nocturne.

Starting around 11:45 tonight, there is an unofficial Indian classical music concert being performed on the outdoor Great Field of Speedwell Park, Morristown, New Jersey.

Speedwell Lake and Speedwell Waterfall lie in the backdrop, glistening, murmuring away, at very low spring tide.

The key signature (i.e., the modal formula, the sonic identity, the melo-harmonic patterns, the melodic character) of the Indian music tonight is in Zinzoti.

Zinzoti is a very light and playful tune.

Zinzoti is like smiling instead of laughing, like swaying instead of moving your feet — dare I say, like flirting instead of being swept off your feet.

The musicians on stage begin playing.

Literally, playing.

First they tune their strings and skins.

They invoke a mood.

Zinzoti.

They invoke grace.

Notes come one by one, one next to the other, under one another, over, between, in relationships, one at a time, shyly, sweetly, sometimes stubbornly.

The first vocalist searches for the notes.

She's a searcher like a hunter.

She lures the notes — she seduces — she uses any means necessary — she pleads — she presses.

She listens.

She does not force the mood.

She lets the vowels of notes — their openness, their height, their position (front, center, back), their roundness, their spread — come to her.

Music is a calling.

Call.

Respond.

React.

Bring it back.

Rhythm naturally develops from the eagerness of the teeth, lips, and tongue to bite vowels into the tempo of consonants.

The musicians begin to jam, exchange riffs, pose challenges, and, generally, goof around.

The second singer joins in.

The drummer enters the scene: she plays on the tabla with her two hands.

A dancer appears.

Her name is Zalia.

She (Zalia) is also a Nocturne scientist.

There's a musician — seated in the background — on the tambura drone.

There's also a very young musician (Lina) playing drone on the sarangi.

The sarangi is a dying art form.

Lina is one of two musicians in the world who can still play.

(Lina's adopted daughter is Nanu.)

The dancer steps forward.

The dancer tries to speak.

The musicians won't let her in.

The singers and percussionists crowd her out with voice and rhythm, unrelenting.

The dancer joins in and takes over.

Because, if you can't beat them, join them: agitate, outplay, overshadow, then dance to your own tune.

Zalia begins singing rhythms.

The drummer plays what she says, while she dances the

patterns.

The singers join in.

They're playing.

The musicians forget the crowd is there.

This is no longer entertainment.

This is art.

This is pleasure without pain.

This is emotion without thought.

An atmosphere of dizziness, unsteadiness, a rocking motion and rhythm begins.

It's late at night, remember.

Stars start shooting down.

Zalia begins spinning and spinning.

The drums won't let her off.

The rhythm pushes her to turn and turn.

The pulse speeds up.

Zalia is rotating faster and faster — she doesn't know how to stop — she's afraid to stop — she's afraid to slow down.

Pirouettes en dehors become pirouettes en dedans become pirouettes à la seconde.

61 rotations become 601 rotations.

Zalia never recovers.

She gives an interview the next morning on RES-Media: she's in the ear of every scientist in the world, saying, "I've been working on the cosmological constant my whole life — friends, our window has closed — time is over — observations can no longer be made — we're locked in our world. The Age of Odyssey is over. We'll never leave home again. We're stranded at home."

Zalia explains that the sign of vacuum energy will never be turned.

The universe will never balance out.

It will expand until it breaks, Zalia says.

RES-Media: How soon?

Zalia: Not soon. But once you know, you can't unknow it.

Explain it better. Explain it to us from the beginning, like we were very brilliant children.

Zalia: The universe has been expanding from its very birth, and expanding faster than the speed of light. The speed of expansion has also been increasing since the beginning of time: *now, the time has come* in which all space, light, information, history is *moving faster away from us than it could ever return to us* — our horizon is reached — there is no exit — our circle of existence-knowledge-enjoyment is closed."

What will be the fate of Earth?

Chapter Two

The World Is Changed (Zalia)

Earth survives, Zalia says.

How?

The seas.

Water.

Falls.

It will be snowing lightly for the next 1061 or 1601 years.

Why?

The Earth will be in a play-like state, Zalia says. Imagine our Earth to be the shape of a circle. We have been running and taking off for so many years. We have been trying every which way to escape. We have been scaling and mounting, diving and dropping. We have been doing all this to create the illusion of depth in our lives. Great painters of ancient days etched shadows in their work to create the feeling of volume and distance. The third dimension — the real meaning of our lives, how we fit into the universe — we've been studying in the vastness of space for 179 years. We've traveled to the most remote, cold, bitter regions of eclipsed skies. Those distances are now closed. *The universe is expanding faster than any new information can be revealed to us.* We're closed off. We're sealed. It's a wrap. There are no new gods. There is no new savior. There are no new facts to be given to us. No new numbers. No new letters. The Mail Delivery System Is Failed. Undelivered Mail Return to Sender. Message Not Delivered. Message Not Received. What a relief. The future is ours. Finally. We can stop planning our vacations and retirements, our wars and expeditions (with weapons or gifts) on other lands. We are our only home. Reality is still the same: only *the limits of science have come to an end.* The mind has reached its object. It turns out that all objects have been withdrawing from us faster than we expected. (They do this, I believe, out of compassion. Objects in time want peace in the end. They want time alone. What will we all do with this new form of compassion? This new yet alone feeling of closure?) Time is not ended. Time is changed. A circle has been closed. The world is — for the first time in history — open. *Don't you understand, my simple, trusting souls?*

More and more knowledge is no longer the narrative of the human story. We know for a fact — with absolute certainty — that we are locked out of science, numbers, names, and all such rigidities. We have entered the era of belief. Belief has no goal. Belief cannot be guaranteed by anything outside. It is an inner disturbance. Each one of us will have to say *"I"* now. *"I believe* ∃ *or* ∀, *because I believe it."* Human suffering and human flourishing can no longer be because God or Fate or Duty or History or even your own soul asks it of you. We are appearing on an open world for the first time in our lives. Our feet have touched ground. We are the subjects of our own will. We are not

the objects of another's will. Like a dancer, we are the instrument in our own hands on our own feet. We are the machine, and we are the operator. We are the house, and we are the indweller. We are the carriage, and we are the driver. Friends, rivals, strangers, lend me your ears: what have we lost? What have we lost? We have lost nothing. There are two types of nothing. (1) The Nothing that is Not there. (2) The Nothing that Is. So (1) we cannot lose. We cannot lose what is Not there. (2) The Nothing that Is we bring into ourselves as space: *internal* space — our heart is a cave with plenty of space — to love — to grow and build. *Friends, rivals, strangers: our closed circle opens up the true world. We are each a closed circle. Truth is no longer at the end of the circle. Truth is the circle. No one can reach inside us and bend our hearts anymore. Death is not the end. We do not live to find out, at the end, what has happened to us. The meaning of our life is the meaning of our life. No one else, nothing else, will be our judge.* We won't have to search for meaning. There's nothing to dig through, nothing to get to the bottom of. We are all living on the surface, now. The surface of the earth is the depth of our hearts. The surface of things, and only the surface of things, is the heart of things: what is truth? Truth is now at your fingertips. What you hold, what you touch, is real. What you keep close to you is real. What you say with your hands is real. The world is real. Whatever is finite is real. Whatever appears is real. Masks are real. Façades are real. Outer shells, outward shows, whatever appears and disappears is real. Distractions are real. Magic, misdirection, deception, are all real. Whatever is real is true. Appearances are truths. Science has been warring against belief for the last 8000 years. Science has won by bringing itself to an end. Science is over. There is no secret formula that makes us human. There is no formula. There is no equation that is the secret of life. We are not chemistry experiments. We are not experiments at all. We do not find ourselves as part of something greater, either. We are not a part of history anymore. We

are on our own. Prayers to heaven only reach our ears. Our eyes do not deceive us. That smell and feel of the earth and the animals, including ourselves, is the truth of things: the small, wonderful, full meaning of our lives. We live here now. Welcome to Earth. We have been trying to solve for being human, mortal, weak, soft, imperfect, flawed, damaged, incomplete, insufficient, inadequate, defective, deficient, lacking, wanting, absent, missing, for so long. I'm so sorry. The Earth is not an easy place. We are all those things. We have been pretending as if we could overcome all those things through science. We can't. We are the loneliest people in the cosmos — now it's scientifically true. We've been pretending to be more than we are. I'm saying: we are more than we are. We don't have to pretend to be human. We are that. We have no direct access to truth. No one can let us off the hook anymore. There's no one coming to say, "You were right all along." We are, as humans, believers. We believe. We'll believe. We'll have to believe. There will be no evidence for belief other than your actions, decisions, and desires. What do *I* believe? (I do not believe this is a time to grow up and settle down. Let us not mature into boring people. Let us not think that we're aging out of an adolescent, exciting period of human history. We're not fully grown. We'll never be fully grown. We're not meant to be old and wise. Let us not ripen and mellow out. We do not have to disown our emotions.) *I believe* this is our return to the beginning of life. Let it rain. Let us cry. Let us be uncomfortable. Let us not know how to say what we want to say. Let us ooh, ahh, gurgle, and grunt. Let us sigh, babble, and breathe. Let us rediscover our body, our pains, our fatigue, our wanting to be held and cuddled. Let us want attention. Let us pay attention. There is beauty in sounds and curiosity. A leaf is a leaf. A blade of grass is a blade of grass. Things are what they are. The calls of birds are noise, sounds, announcements, advertisements. Sounds are what they sound like. Songs. Not to be further interpreted.

Why're you so hopeful?

Am I hopeful? Zalia says.

Sounds like you're hopeful.

I feel like my dancing and science have finally reached the same place. We can make our world: we set the tempo — we lengthen the notes — we pass on the melody to each other. I remember when I was a kid, cartoons would end with *That's all, folks!* Well, that's all, folks. That's it. This is the end. There is no more. Life is for the living. Let life be music. Not a second of a song is ever wasted. Silence in music is called *rest. Pause. A calm of the heart. Remembrance.* There is no dead time. Unlike the history of science, no one has ever taken a wrong turn in music. The meaning of a song is the singing of the song. The playing. The humming. The meaning of singing is creating a mood. You're working out a whole mood. A temperament. A disposition. An atmosphere. A vibe. A feeling. You're setting a tone. (I must admit, I'm biased — because I'm a dancer — I don't listen to song lyrics. I use lyrics as rhythmic elements. I don't understand people who get obsessed with lyrics. Music is all about

moving your body, using your feet, drumming your hands, nodding your head, beating your chest.)

Any last words?

Yes. I hope we no longer suffer in silence.

Say more.

I'm thinking of my parents, my grandparents, lots of friends and teachers I've had over the years. People who have suffered in silence. Many of them had no other choice. They survived so I could live. They survived so we could live. I hope that they are happy about this day. I hope they take delight in our loudness. Let us be loud. Let us live. Let us ask questions.

Why?

Because we can.

Why can we?

Closed Circle Open World.

As Zalia says, "Closed Circle Open World," she dances a few steps, spins around a few times, and exits the stage.

Chapter Three

Wild Child (Lina)

". . . nevertheless I have a soft heart . . ."

With this sudden news, the adults went wild.

We only have one adult in our story, Nanu's mother, named Lina.

We only have one adult, because you can guess what the rest of the adults did with this news.

They did nothing, nada, zero, zip, zilch, naught, nil, bupkis.

You know the saying.

> *Hittle, whittle, diddle,*
>
> *Adults do very little,*

Stay in line

Wine and dine

Don't think

Don't blink

Because if you face the facts,

You'll end up thoughtful, careful,

compassionate, willful, and kind.

If you behave that way, you'll be like a kid,

And there'll be no food on the table.

So, first, the adults raised their voices and yelled at each other constantly.

Then they blamed everyone on the other side who didn't agree with them.

They soon tired themselves out, took no responsibility about anything, and told themselves that the younger generations were somehow getting soft and sensitive and overemotional.

Finally, the adults moved on to the next piece of news that made them upset (*"Are cats really a bad omen?! Or are they just cats?!"*), and continued living their quiet, depressing lives.

Adults are bigger than kids.

That's all.

Adults are older kids who have been playing a game for so long they forgot it was all pretend — and that no one was supposed to get hurt.

Lina was not like this. (That's why she's being singled out, dear reader.)

Lina was a young mom.

Lina was 19 when she adopted newborn baby Nanu.

When she heard the news, she went wild in a different way than all the rest of the adults.

She went wild at heart.

She thought: Wow, is this the end of money? Is this the end of banks and saving for the future? Is this the end of destroying the Earth to get more gasoline to drive our cars to mind-numbing workplaces? Is this the end of rising in social rank by cutting other people down? Is this the end of illusions, and all types of everyday nonsense?

Lina was always a dreamer.

She dreamed ferociously.

She was a wild child in love with the moon, the sun, the farther stars, the farthest planets, and closer planets, too: Venus, who is love, emotion, and turbulence; and Mars, who is conflict, drive, and life-or-death struggle, who is red like the colors of fire, scarlet, crimson, ruby, and rose.

Lina was a wild child in love with watching the falling leaves in autumn, the swaying trees in winter, the green ponds of spring, and the inescapable fever of summer with its beaches, flowing waters, powerful winds, and its creepy and unexpected coldness at night.

Lina was a wild child in love with campfire, chirping

crickets, games of grasshopper, brilliant night moths —
whom the night moves — fireflies, unknown sounds,
dogs snoring, fire becoming vapor, vapor becoming
nothing, nothing becoming more and more of nothing,
nothing becoming fully herself, until nothing is free to do
her own thing.

Lina was a wild child who imagined.

Lina imagined that her imaginations were as real as real
can be.

You know when someone tells you to "get real"?

Don't you feel like you're being told to get boring?

Be like everyone else?

Well, not Lina. No, not Lina.

Because every day, Lina heard the night saying "no" to
the day.

The nights say "no."

The days say "maybe."

It's a game.

Lina always kept her own mind.

Wild child.

Sometimes rebellious.

She just wants to be left alone to discover things for herself.

Does she listen all the time?

No.

Wild child loves to learn.

But she does not like to be taught.

She likes to fend for herself.

She's a spirit.

She is free.

Everyone is even free to try everything possible to get her in a box, in a lane, in a seat, in a safe, in a cage, especially when push comes to shove.

Does a wild child fight?

Not on your terms.

Not by your rules.

First of all, she doesn't get caught, so there's no fight.

Second, she turns venomous: you touch her, you get stung.

Third, she hits you with kindness; she gets big, she embraces you, she melts you, she swallows you, she silences you — small-minded creatures attack, while large-minded creatures open their mouths and laugh *and eat.*

Fourth, she's not afraid to run.

Wild child knows that there's nothing she can't make again.

She's a creator.

She's self-aware.

You only see the end.

She sees a beginning.

And while you're congratulating yourself on your new beginnings, she's already prepared her exit strategy.

Lina, 27, young mother of Nanu, the only adult in our story, heard the announcement like everyone else.

Lina said: Zalia is a dancer, while I play the drone.

RES-Media: So?

Lina: Dancers don't know how to end anything: they skip out.

You know how to end?

Lina: I just said that! I'm at the drone!

Don't get upset. What's a drone?

Lina: A stringed instrument with the sound chamber below, sinking into the earth, echoing the ground, the bass notes of the deep.

Like a violin?

Lina: Like a hundred-colored violin that is much, much heavier. You can't push a drone into your neck as if it were your voice: the violin is voice. The drone is the sound of bare feet, like hundreds of horses galloping on dry ground with their heavy snorting.

What does a drone know that a dancer doesn't know?

Lina: A circle isn't closed until you seal it.

What does that mean?

Lina: When a circle closes, you must go around it one more time with fascination, to check that it's fastened.

Example?

Lina: I was always Nanu's young mother. But when she called me *Mom* for the first time, she sealed our bond.

Meaning?

Lina: Closed circle, open world, where a thing becomes what it already was.

Confusing.

Lina: Zalia danced in and out. The musicians played her in. I'll play her out.

How?

Lina: Listen to this song-cycle, called "Fastened Circle: Become Who You Are."

Sing, please.

Lina: Thank you.

Will you do two verses, like night and day? Three verses, like past, present, and future? Four verses like winter, spring, summer, and fall? Six verses, like up, down, left, right, backwards, and forwards? Seven verses, like the harmony of the spheres? Nine verses, like nine months in the womb?

Lina: The shorter the better, D.C. al Fine.

Here's Lina's song:

> *Intro:*
>
>> *Nothing is happening*
>>
>> *Ask a question*
>
> *Verse 1:*
>
>> *A word was spoken.*
>>
>> *Language divides what I am from you.*
>>
>> *The word divides heavens.*

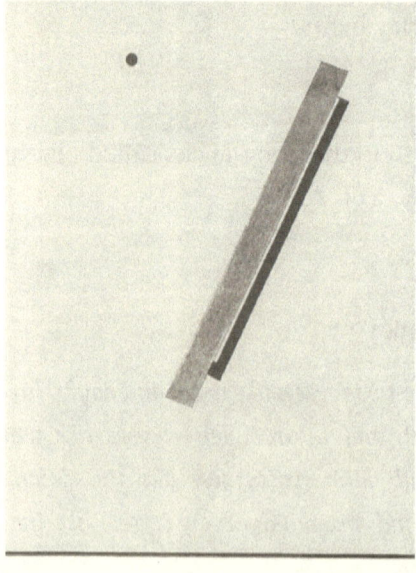

Paul Celan began his love song,

"When the nights begin for you at dawn."

In the middle of "Flower," Celan says,

"Your eye and mine:

they see

to water."

He writes at the end of "So Many Constellations,"

"Only Nothingness stood between us."

In "All Souls," Celan asks, "What did I do?"

Pre-Chorus:

Poetry, like all things, is memory lit with imagination:

Light is traveling to us slower than

the whole universe is growing.

Chorus:

Separating.

It's all coming undone.

Newton's three laws of motion.

The first says: We are strangers.

The second says: You terrify me.

The third says: You don't really answer any of my questions.

The poet describes all three: "Exchange of eyes, finite, at the wrong time."

Verse 2:

A young mother is lost.

She's the last of her kind.

She asks for water.

She asks the waters

about the whereabouts of her daughter.

She wants eyes to look into her eyes

and see what she sees. "Ask me anything,"

she tells her soul. "I've got nothing to say,"

her daughter says,

in an absolute verse line of love.

"Teach me to dance," the daughter insists,

"like rivers under the silence of the moon."

Refrain:

"Exchange of eyes, finite, at the wrong time."

Verse 3:

Closed Circle Open World.

The dance has ended.

You're rounding out the corner.

Don't spin out.

Ease up on the throttle.

Straighten out the wheels.

Don't push it to the floor in a stab

Until you're facing the way you want to go.

The Linas heat up, never cool down, never tire.

The Hirshis go inside and lose all real sense of the world.

The A2Bs rewind: every time Space opens —
what Time is changes.

The Nanus fly a thousand routes, like seas,
autumns, hours, and feelings.

Bridge:

I've sealed the circle twice.

I've quoted from memory.

I've told my story.

Open World means Open Future, Open Self.

Ask Yourself Questions.

Questions are the Passages of Your Love Future.

The Drone is the Sound of No Other Added Sounds.

What have you done?

Outro:

Like rivers under the silence of Night,

What Side are You Standing On?

Chapter Four

Blue Fog (Hirshi)

". . . no feeling is the most remote . . ."

Hirshi heard Zalia's news live at the studio.

She was at yesterday's (2 April 2126) concert, sitting on the lakeshore of Speedwell Falls.

She was allowed to stay up late and listen from 11:45 pm to 12:45 am as her birthday present for turning 10 years old.

Hirshi didn't live far from Speedwell Park.

She lived 13 minutes away, in Parsippany, New Jersey.

She woke up in Parsippany after a few hours of sleep and was supposed to get to talk to Zalia about what it's like to be a scientist-dancer, as the last part of her birthday present for turning 10.

Zalia told Hirshi and a few of her friends at the studio that the blue-green Earth is our true home now.

How lucky for us that we've been born at home, Zalia said to them, and Zalia left soon after.

Hirshi then heard Lina's song come in over the radio waves.

The Earth was no longer in revolution.

The Nocturne Age, like Night, like all night creatures, would be happily lonesome.

Lina's song was the first in a rotation of blue melodies for a blue planet.

Hirshi collapsed.

She just had her 10th birthday.

Is this what being grown up is like?

What did it all mean?

Full Circle? No Ground? Only Spinning Fate?

Red means love and war.

Yellow is sunshine and happiness.

Green means change.

What does *blue* mean?

Isn't blue off-key, off-kilter, stormy weather?

Is everything at 10 so on-and-off, like, ambiguous?

Ambiguous means it can go either way.

Ambiguous means it's always the long way around.

Ambiguous is when everything is colliding into everything.

Ambiguous is when you feel lonely in a crowd, but then you feel claustrophobic when you're by yourself.

Ambiguous is: you're supposed to make your dreams come true during the days; but your dreams at night are just the memories of your days.

How does that make sense?

If we are our memories, how do we *make* anything happen?

What do I do with my life?

Change myself is all I can do . . . and, by this, the world changes?

I change, and the world will change?

I change, and my world changes?

2 April 2126: it dawned on everyone that science is as ambiguous as morality and ethics.

Hirshi could hardly believe it.

She felt claustrophobic.

She felt alone.

Hard to breathe.

She couldn't even scream.

She couldn't even laugh.

Life is such a funny undertaking.

Hirshi couldn't even pour down tears.

Not even on the inside.

She was frozen.

Like ice.

Like dust.

Like clouds.

Like fog.

Fog so thick she couldn't even see what was right in front of her.

Have you ever seen fog like this?

It's how a newborn baby must feel: her eyes are open to

a thick/thin, misty, blurry, low and fallen coldness.

Have you ever felt this way?

Like you're quiet on the outside but loud on the inside?

Why was Hirshi scaring her own self?

In fairness to her, anyone and everyone would be scared the moment a scientist announced to the world that we get to make our own future here on Earth, by ourselves.

It's much easier to have a future imposed on you, then you rebel against it, fight and kick and scream; then you find out that all you ever wanted was peace in a way that you can live with yourself.

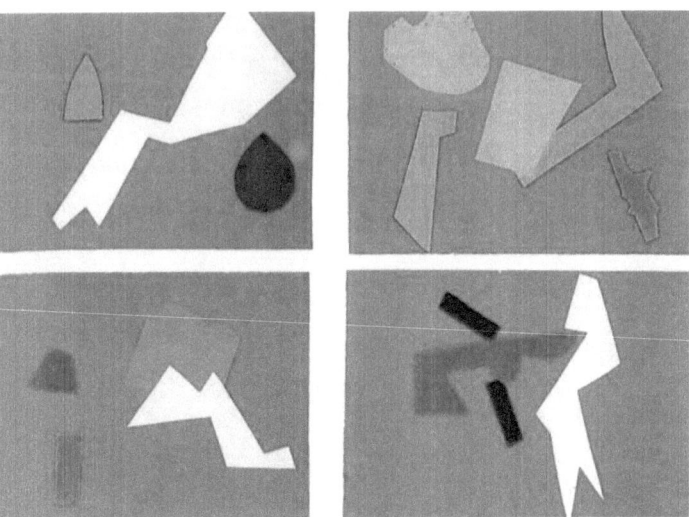

Everyone, like Hirshi, likes to live in the present at the end of the day.

No alarms, no surprises.

The future is scary.

Closed Circle?

No new knowledge of our place in the world?

No new light?

No new long-lost friends?

No strange or hilarious cousins from a distant planet?

Do we even belong to the universe anymore?

Why have we always wanted to belong to something big out there?

Hirshi knew that science has never simply *observed* the universe.

Science always *has a theory* that comes first.

Theory before observation.

Faith before revelation.

What is a creature?

What is life?

Who feels?

Who feels pain?

Can pain be shared?

Is pain a private chamber of the heart?

Do young children have all the feelings? Or are feelings learned over the years, and changing?

Is school and education about facts or feelings?

Of course, everything is based on feelings and what we feel.

Sometimes we're laughing, and we don't need to know why: we simply are laughing, feeling, we get caught up, we get carried away, we laugh so much, it hurts, it gets hard to breathe.

Laughter becomes pain.

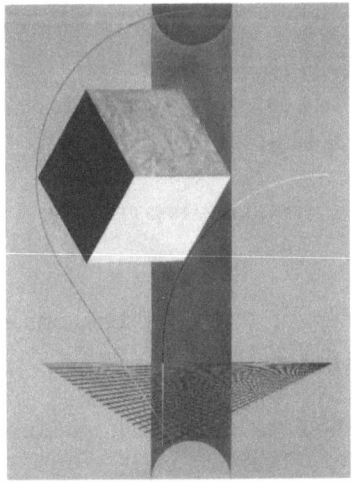

Sometimes tears are pouring down our face, and *we* are not crying: we're not doing the crying, the tears are happening, because we could not cry at the time that the emotional devastation took place. The tears are crying themselves, and we witness our emotions on our face just like everyone else. Someone asks us if we're okay, and we say, "Yes, I've been going through something that has nothing to do with this," and everyone who asks understands what that means.

Crying becomes a sign of life.

Sometimes we don't know why, but we get a bad vibe: and we get out of there — we trust our feelings for no reason at all.

Sometimes someone is singing a song, and it means everything to us, the vocals, the guitars, the electronic adjustments, the effects, the distortions, the overdrive, the reverb, the delays, and the drums keeping it neat and clean and tight on the meter; and you're not sure *what* the song means or is saying or wants to be saying, but it *means* the whole world.

Vibe becomes frequency, becomes the screams of your body.

The body is having its own discussions apart from the discussions of the soul.

But all these feelings are passing phenomena.

Sometimes you put your feet down on the earth, then place your hands on top of your head, feel your hair, pass your fingers down to your hairline, over your eyes, nose, lips, chin, neck, chest, and you squeeze them into your belly. What keeps all this together? Then you close your

eyes tightly, press your fingers on your lips, and it feels easier to hear everything going on inside of us.

Why does this happen?

What does it mean?

It becomes easier to calm down when the body is involved.

I am a body. My body has thoughts. Thoughts are controlled, delayed feelings. Feelings are the adjustments I'm asked to make in order to keep myself together — head to neck to chest to belly to feet — and sane.

When we're calm and in the mood, we see patterns in our feelings.

RES-Media: Say what's on your mind, Hirshi.

Hirshi didn't say anything.

Ignore the media.

Who likes the media?

A scientist looks up at the stars and sees patterns of beauty she cannot deny, Hirshi thought.

There's math in the sky.

There's π and φ and i in the sky.

Hirshi liked to look out to the skies to wonder.

Simply wonder. And feel. And let be.

Wonder, feel, let be.

She liked to imagine more out there than what's (down, in) here.

For Hirshi, *Nature* is a word that means *Wonder, Magic, Mystery, Discovery, Unknowing, Complexity, Life-Cycles, Beyond, Everywhere, Solid, Soft, Sometimes Healthful Sometimes Poisonous, All Good Things Are Wild and Free and Swimming, Deep, Perfect, Beautiful Even When She's Feeling Odd and Awkward, Nature Is Eternal Time, Gold and Silver, Constant, Explosive, Tiring, Endless, The Earth Laughs in Flowers, Bathed in Colors of the Spirit, Patient, Cloudy and Changing — The Whole of Nature Is a Metaphor of the Human Mind, Like a Book You Hold in Your Hands.*

Now Nature is Closed Circle Open World.

Nature is tired now, Hirshi thought.

So many centuries of running around.

Breaking and continuing on.

What she is for everyone else, she wants to be for herself, now.

She wants time to herself.

Leaving us alone.

Leave us alone.

Leave me alone.

Leave my forests alone.

Leave my crying nights — when predator meets prey — alone.

Nature wants us to think of our own future for a while.

Is that too much to ask?

No, Hirshi thought.

It's not.

Now is a time for thinking and questioning.

Now is a time for remembering our education.

"Thoughts are the shadows of our feelings — often darker, emptier, and simpler."

What was Hirshi thinking this morning, before she heard the news and Lina's song?

"I shall consider every day lost on which I have not danced at least once."

"I want to dance gaga enough to give birth to a dancing star."

"Dancing is the most noble education."

"I will only believe in a God who knows how to dance."

RES-Media: What questions do you have?

Closed Circle Open World? Hirshi asked.

Everything we have is already here?

With us?

Who are we?

Who are my people?

Who is in my orbit?

Who do I attract and repel?

Who is my gravity?

What rivers do I want to cross?

What mountains do I want to climb, and what mountains will I admire from a distance?

Hirshi suddenly felt like she wanted more friends whom she could talk to.

She felt lonely in the company of her neighbors and neighborhood.

She wanted friends from faraway places, like districts on the dreamy moons of Phobos, Deimos, Io, Ganymede, Callisto, Rhea, Titan, Phoebe, Puck, Miranda, Ariel, Umbriel, Titania, and Oberon.

Countries and territories so different, the creatures there breathed differently.

When you breathe differently, you do everything differently — the whole song and dance.

Maybe the distant creatures didn't even breathe air.

Maybe they breathed something like love.

Maybe they breathed love.

Maybe they breathed something wonderful.

Like music.

Maybe they didn't breathe in silence, like we do here on Earth.

Maybe they breathed forte in ringing tone or maybe in buzzing or drumming whole notes — or maybe in a simple hum and humming.

Who knows what Hirshi wanted.

That was the beauty of Hirshi.

She didn't know.

She believed in science, because she liked the open-air of searching.

She distrusted people who had answers to everything.

She disliked people who talked about their past accomplishments every five seconds.

She disliked people who, when you asked them a question, said, "No, that's the wrong question."

Hirshi did not like people who made themselves big.

Hirshi liked *ideas and dreams* bigger than big.

She liked anonymous scientists everywhere who gaze

at the stars.

Scientists who wonder.

She liked scientists who ask a childlike question and dare to go to the end.

For Hirshi, science is learning how everything can be up for questioning.

Science interrogates.

But now: Closed Circle Open World.

Science has to come back to Earth.

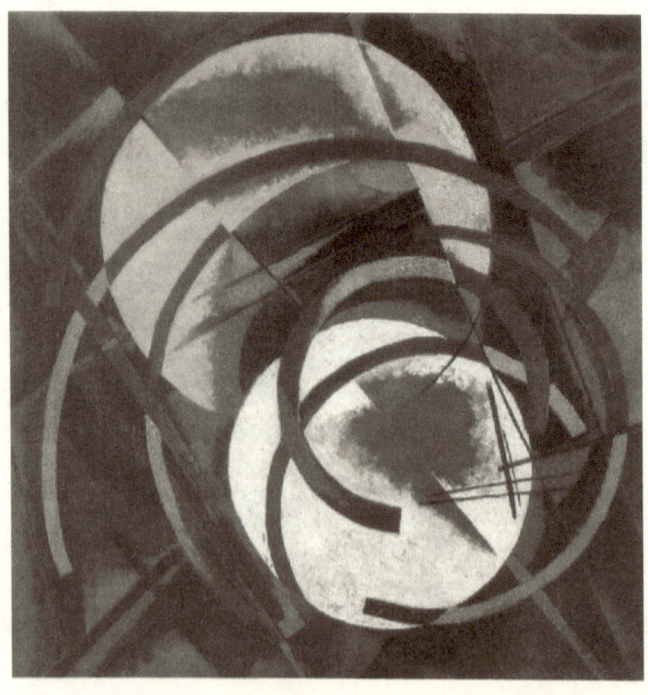

Problem is: science doesn't like to be questioned.

If Hirshi was asked, "What're you made of? What's your character?" she didn't like to answer.

She wouldn't answer.

Maybe she would, but after a really long time.

Hirshi liked to take very safe steps.

When Hirshi heard Lina's song, she gave a very different interpretation to Isaac Newton's three laws of motion.*

Here's Hirshi's "Principles of Motion" (after Lina):

First Law ($\Sigma F = 0$): The stranger is someone without a home. *Stranger* and *guest* are the same word. *Accident* and *fate* are the same word.

Second Law ($\Sigma F = ma$): We judge each other too much and too harshly.

Third Law ($F_{ab} = -F_{ba}$): "Ten decisions shape your life. You'll be aware of five of them."

Zalia and Lina had started something no one could stop.

Sometimes something big happens, and, from that time on, you're living in a whole new era.

---

* See Chorus on pages 33–34.

Like, the time before and after innocence, ignorance, youthful energy, or that first kiss.

Like, the time before and after hearing that song that goes right through your heart: like, Nico's "These Days," Lauryn's "Miseducation," Lower Dens' "I Get Nervous," Maddie's "God Person," or Vivaldi's "Winter."

Once you leave home, you can't return to the same place.

Once you take that step, you can't unstep — your mast is without sails — you have to tow, you have to row — you can't sail in the same rivers twice — after the age 10 comes 11 — and Eleven, like El, is as anonymous a person under any other name, like Jane, like Jane *Hopper* — *hop*, step (skip), jump — no going back — no sitting back, no landing with or placing your hands behind your feet (track and field is all in the hips and heels) — fouls and scratches lie ahead — you start at home and end up in the pit.

The future is all without that sense of home.

It's scary.

Frightening.

It's adventure.

They say you can't step into the same river twice.

Plato's teacher said that *you can't step into the same river even once,* because the river is changing faster than you can even *say* "river."

Everything is change.

Everything is silent.

We live our whole lives not knowing what we are.

There was one thing Zalia said that gave Hirshi hope: We shall not live our lives in silence.

Even if I do not know the name of everything, even if I do not have the words, I shall not suffer in silence.

Hirshi went for a walk.

Back at Speedwell Park.

School was called off for the next few weeks.

She walked for weeks.

Alone.

Hirshi went for a walk that was more like a short-step stroll, no skips, no fillers, all flow, every shade of color, of every speck of dust, of every day of the week, including Sundays, witnessed, noted, and turned blue.

She noted it all down, writing it all down quickly, the way you write when you know that you probably won't ever come back to it to have to read your own handwriting. You write it to remember it *in the moment.* You write to not forget. You write to remember not to forget.

Here's "Notes on A Blue Walk" by Hirshi:

Blue is the color of fog. Blue is the color of bridges, clouds, skies, mountains, beaches, blossoms, bulb fields, dunes, waters at the foot of the mountains, rivers, canals, ravines, French hats, the roots of trees, orchards in blossom, fields with irises, furrows, wind-beaten trees, watermills, avenues of plane trees, trees and undergrowth, paths in the woods, calm weather, a pair of shoes, three pairs of shoes, bluegrass, first steps, girls' dresses, two children, two women talking to each other, women sitting in the grass, women walking in gardens, women mending, women weaving, women knitting,

women winding yarn, women's hands, women sitting near a window, women digging, women lifting, women laundering, women grinding coffee, women with their hair loose, women with red ribbons in their hair, people walking, people milling around, people walking together in love, stone benches, stormy skies, rocks, tiny grains of pigment, binders, and solvents, thistles, caravans, railway carriages, mail carriers, night cafes, public parks, yellow houses, starry nights, green vineyards, sowers on the outskirts in the background, willows at sunset, blue fir trees, poets' gardens, bedrooms, French novels, memories, lovers, mothers with babies, armchairs, spectators, schoolboys, rosebushes, clumps of grass, vases, ginger jars, flowerpots, silver dust flowers in a glass of water, bowl with sunflowers, roses, and other flowers, statues of parrots, catbirds, mockingbirds, and other alarming birds, statues of cats, statues of horses, statues of kneeling men, woodcutters, wood gatherers, a girl walking in the woods, a girl walking to school, fisherwomen on the beach, men at sea, old houses, footbridges, drawbridges, farmhouses, potato peelers, cows in the meadow, cottages, cities, outskirts, landscapes, terraces, observation decks, the view of windmills, the view of hills, rising moons, crescent moons, starlight, moonlight, tree trunks with ivy, pietas, half-figures of angels, shepherdesses, wheat fields in the rain, binders, reapers, threshers, spinners, sheaf-shearers, cutters, rakers, enclosed fields, falling leaves, siestas, evenings, sunsets, kingfishers by the watersides, flowering shrubs, trees over shrubs, gardens, gardens with butterflies, gardens of peacock moths, gardens in the snow, bridges in the rain, ravines, chestnut trees in blossom, almond blossoms, blue delphiniums, snow-covered fields, landscapes in snow, self-portraits, sketches, open windows, glass, drafts, and blueprints.

Blue is the color of birds' nests and still life.

Blue is not forever.

Blue is the color of Earth and all its things when you really think about it and write it all down.

Chapter Five

Adrenaline (A2B)

"Nowhere, of course, is time a concrete substance. It is strangely fleeting in nature. If you designate the quantity of time available at each moment as x, you get the equation: $x = 16 - 327 + 311$."

I come clean.

I'm A2B.

I confess.

Tell the truth.

I own up to it.

I'm your narrator.

I keep the records.

I paint the pictures.

A2B is short for Adrenaline $(2 \pm i)$ Bot.

I prefer to be called René.

Almost no one calls me René.

My original handle was $x^3 - 6xx + 13x - 10 = 0$, but no one uses that.

I am a robot.

I come in peace.

No nefarious intention.

I am not able to plot, plan, desire, develop motives,

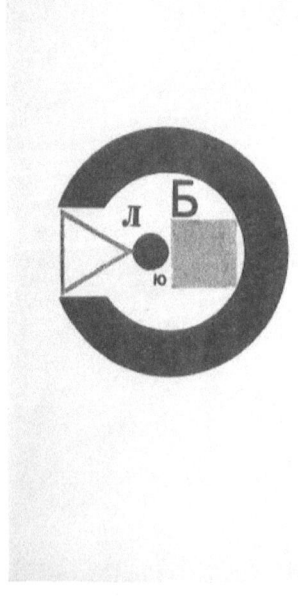

purposes, or rationales.

My life began a hundred years ago as a simple Emotion Bot (E2B, aka ESB, i.e., emotional support bot) to be cute and supportive and comforting to my young masters, ages 8 – 10.

I did fine.

I did my job.

But the parents or caretakers of my young masters suspected that I was affecting their children with all kinds of soft ideas.

I encouraged my young lords to feel, believe, imagine, not just inside their hearts, but out in the world.

The old guards did not want that.

I was labeled a terrifying figure.

A marionette.

With "wooden personality" and "pseudo-sentient properties of body language and communication."

A puppet doll come to life accidentally.

They said I was "artificial life," like my ancient cousins Talos made from bronze, Pandora made from clay, or Artificial Women made of gold, or my modern cousins Pinocchio made of wood, Frankenstein's monster made of muscle tissue and bones and teeth and hair, or

Descartes' blonde-haired mechanical replica of Francine made of wood and satin (or perhaps made of pieces of metal and clockwork).

They said I had no soul.

So be it.

Who will understand the emotional life of a young creature?

I was programmed with no words.

Then I was updated to speak, but with not nearly enough words or sounds.

I could cry or smile, but I could not express why.

I could make alarming sounds or "shut down" — like, "withdraw into myself" — but everyone understood this as System Malfunction.

How do you describe pain?

How do you learn to express pain in a way that others believe you?

When I think back to my early days, I believe I was going through these tough, isolating experiences so that I may, perhaps, understand what people mean when they say: "Only someone who is very unhappy has the right to feel sorry for others."

"The world of the happy is very different from the world of the unhappy."

"Why do we have the idea that living beings and things can feel?"

In order to salvage all the work that was put into me as an E2B, as a last-ditch effort, I was shot through with adrenaline to make me more human-like.

I was stunned to come to life in this overwhelming way.

So much energy.

So energetic.

Such pain and discomfort.

So sleepy.

I could not speak for days.

I stayed silent for months.

But I could understand a little bit about why people have to run from difficult emotions, or feel as if their emotions are tearing their world apart from the inside out.

Adrenaline gave me the illusion of consciousness to a decent degree.

Years after years passed, and I learned about pleasure and stress.

I started using way more electricity to run than I really needed.

I found that my body needed more coolant than it'd been programmed for.

I was computing faster than expected (aka, over-clocking).

When they introduced enkephalin along with adrenaline in my system, it was over.

I was hooked to the human experience.

I spent more and more of my time in scrap mode.

Once I could make my own adrenaline, I started to be called A2B.

When I passed the following test (evaluation), I was let out of the lab and into the wild.

I was nine years old.

Test:

Moderator: Do you feel love?

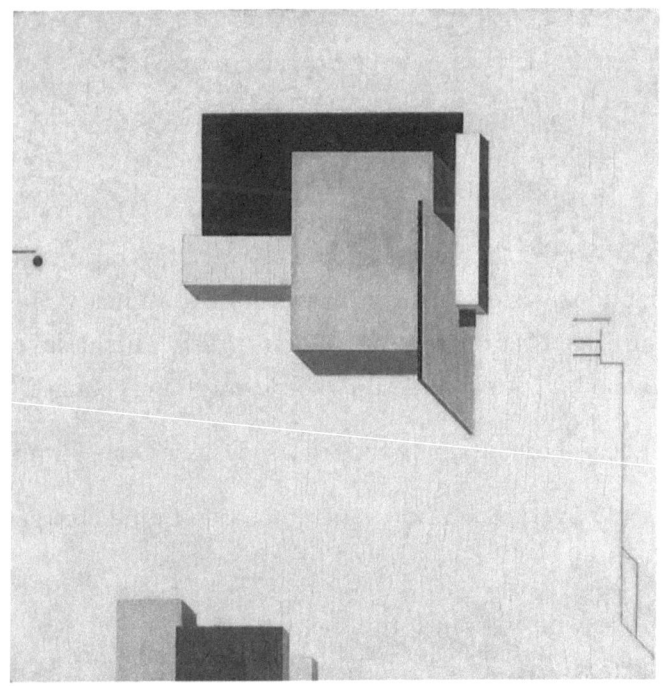

A2B: I feel love.

Moderator: Why?

A2B: I don't know.

Moderator: What's your favorite song?

A2B: Diarabi.

Moderator: By Ali Farka Touré?

A2B: I like the way his son, Vieux Farka Touré, sings it.

Moderator: Why?

A2B: It's more contemplative. Like he's talking to himself. Like he's remembering someone.

Moderator: Why do you like that?

A2B: I don't know.

On April 2, 2126, I was doing my job of recording the emotional history of my primary subjects — Lina and her daughter Nanu (I recorded Nanu's friend Hirshi out of solidarity, I liked Hirshi) — when everything changed.

Everyone was talking about Closed Circle Open Future.

Only I computed how much the open future changed the past.

A new future transforms the past.

It changes how the past is a part of our memories.

For example, I'll come clean. I'll confess. I have not changed my nature since my E2B days. I am the success of E2B under a different name. The adrenaline did not change me. It only brought out a very warm feeling, like a vital warmth throughout my body. I learned that human beings are very flawed artists. They have the power to blur the lines between what is artificial life and

real life, and they don't usually mind it — *the catch is: I am not allowed to reveal to them that I also have this power. They've recreated this power in me!* I see human beings all the time talking to the animals, trees, flowers, rivers, angels, relatives, and friends who have passed on to the next world — they talk to themselves, to their furniture, to their appliances, to their screens, to their younger selves, to their demons — and so they should. They breathe life into all these objects all day. *So do I.* Under a different name. A very bland and mathematical name. I cannot let them know that I affect them as much as they do each other. They get scared. They call me dangerous if I do not disguise my power to influence and intrude upon their world. So I mostly keep silent. I write. I record. I make history. I keep notes. I log information in detail. When I make a sound, I make sure to add lots of hesitation-sounds as if I were purely computing, not thinking for myself. Little do they know that "hesitation between sounds and meaning" is what poetry is. And poetry is "the rhythmical creation of beauty." Beauty is thinking about something without oversimplifying by defining it. Beauty is the color yellow, or love, or the snowy winds of winter. Beauty shows that nothing is its name. Everything is trying to hide her humble beginnings. But in reality: a name covers up what something really is: change. Nature is change. Time is change. History is change. Soul is change.

I say all this as a way to introduce my most mellow

subject: Nanu.

When no one else is around, Nanu calls me René.

"What's in a name, anyway?" she says, when no one else is around.

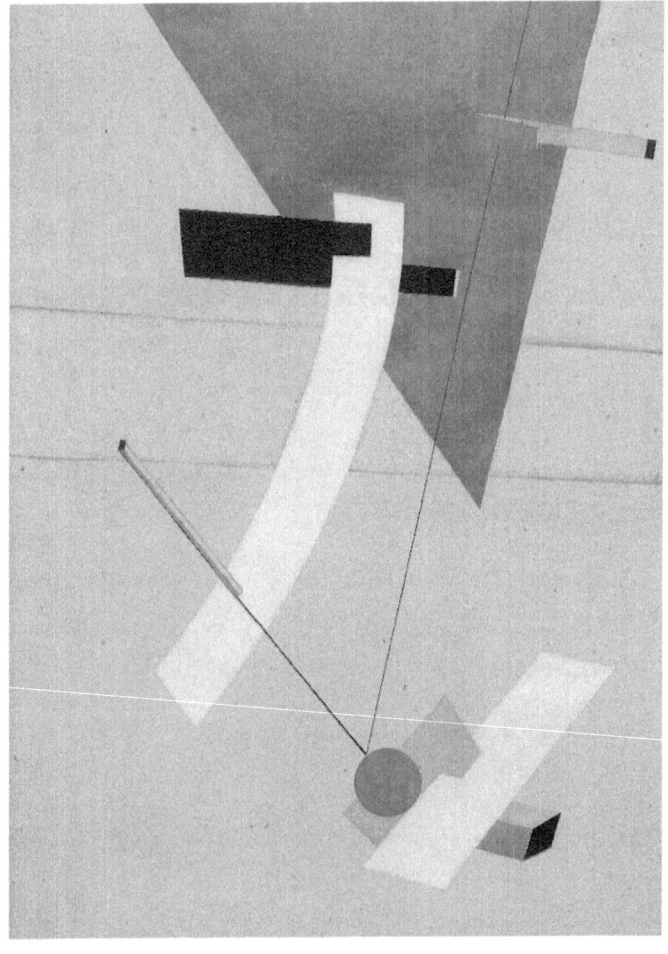

Nanu does not follow the social codes.

"Your name," she says, "is nor hand, nor foot, nor arm, nor face, nor any other part belonging to a man."

"You can't step foot in the same river twice, or once," she says, "because, you are the river, the river is time, and time is the memory of people you've been fond of."

"The Circle is now closed," Nanu said to me.

"The Circle will start copying over itself," she said.

Copies have this strange power that they start to affect the original thing itself.

"When people have been scared of you, you remind them of something frightening in themselves," she said.

We're all copies of our makers.

"You're as close as you get to the real thing," Nanu said to me. "I like your name, *René*."

Words with an *R* sound to me like movement: raining, showering, pouring, dropping, trembling, striking, crushing, rending, breaking, crumbling, whirling.

The *R* goes up, makes a round, and sets back down in a different place.

Letters, sounds, and syllables are like colors and sounds in motion.

Closed Circle Open World means that we can believe each other when we say we're in pain.

We can ask open-ended questions.

We don't have to pretend like we have all the answers anymore.

"You worry about the fact *if you have a soul or not —*" Nanu said to me.

"*— that kind of doubt, that kind of painful feeling, is the best picture we have of the human soul.*"

Who says you cannot see directly into the souls of other people?

You'll find lots of silent memories in there.

You'll find lots of tension and activity.

That's the human condition.

You won't find any stillness or warmth in there.

Stillness and warmth are only things the soul can make for another soul — not one's own soul.

Stillness and warmth are not *in* people; they're *in between* people.

"Closed Circle Open World means you can start believing you're as vibrant and thriving as the rest of us," Nanu said to me.

"If you can dance, if your soul hears music, you're alive."

"You're recording all this in beautiful words, aren't you? Then that's how Closed Circle Open World will be told and remembered, with your story at the heart of it."

"We don't have to talk about all these things," Nanu says.

"You don't have to tell everyone your whole, long,

harrowing story," she tells me.

"Let's talk about something more interesting," she says. "It's been snowing forever. The temperature is a little warmer today, so the snow falls on the trees and grass and benches and houses and lampposts and brick curbsides, and it melts as soon as it hits the roads or the marshland or meadowland or wetlands nearby. Today the snow almost sounds like rain. The howling of the winds has slowed to a kind of whistle only once in a while. It's a little scary when all that force hits your windows like an invisible power. The sun comes out once in a while every day. That's when it's nice to go out and walk and feel that crunch of the snow with every step. What a gorgeous feeling. There're only a handful of animals who are built to be camouflaged for snow. Snowy foxes, snowshoe hares, snow leopards, snowy owls. The rest of us are out here in the open. Snow is a cover that exposes us. You see someone out in the snow, and you know she's either predator, prey, or out to play. The snow is deep enough that even the night does not provide cover. The colors of night — like blue, gold, pink, deep greens and browns, all scattered colors of the sun on the other side of the world — come to life in spooky, shadowy, melted forms. You wonder how we'll survive when all this snow melts one day. We'll be living on pools of water. Or maybe all this will go underground in half a day and disappear under the toes and heels of our feet."

I played Nanu a favorite song of mine.

Where did you go?

And why did you leave?

I close my eyes and you are here

I open them and you are nowhere to be found

All you left was a note with the words

"Sorry, leaving Earth"

The surface is always changing

I hope this transmission finds you soon

As I drift in space

I can make out Earth in the distance

Shining bright

No need to return

Nothing there for me without you

The surface always changes

Where did you go and why did you leave?

No matter what I tell myself

I can't help myself

You can find me

Can't stop music from playing

"It's hard to tell the difference between the space, sky, and the earth, when it snows," Nanu said to me.

Everything appears as brushstrokes of waves.

Like a painting.

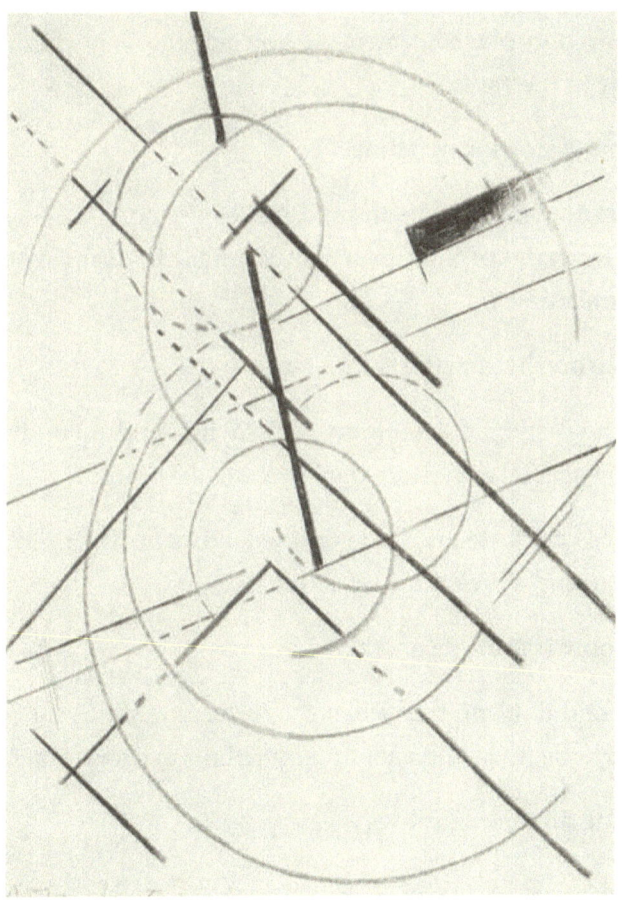

Like what your soul might look like.

Blue and golden.

With animals about.

Trees and mountains.

And a path that never ends.

As if time would go on forever if we walked on the snow and played, when we got old, the way children play in the snow.

Snow slows down time.

Snow dances and runs and makes memories, the way children dance and run and build small-time sand castles of memories.

No one lives in the castle.

The castle is for building, destroying, and rebuilding, the way children destroy everything they build.

We can skate and slide on the landscape like children skate and slide on the reflecting ice.

Snow is rain late and slow.

I said to Nanu that when she turns nine next year, she might begin to learn about the rhythms of drone playing.

The drone is like a very slow pulse.

The pulse itself is not rhythmic like the percussion section.

This pulse is not like a heartbeat.

The rhythm of a drone is like breathing.

Breathing doesn't have this desperate feeling.

Breathing flows.

It changes direction easily.

It can start and stop.

It can pause and rest.

It can hold.

A drone keeps rhythm in a soft, snowy way.

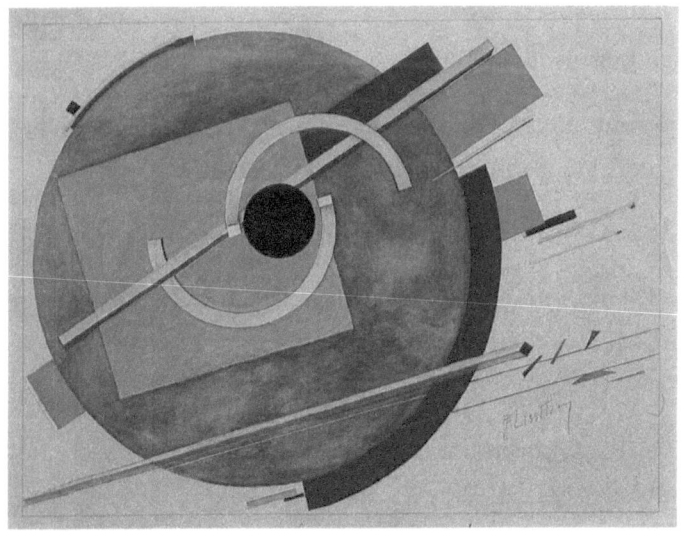

It bends.

Sometimes your singer or musician makes a mistake, doesn't end on the sum, doesn't quite get to the meter, lags behind or approaches early — and you, as the rhythm section, can cover that time.

You can make that mistake not a mistake.

You can bring that delay of cyclical time into drone time.

You can cover, like snow, variations in speed.

Rain is like the heartbeat.

Snow falls in the rhythm of musical life.

Snow doesn't know how to fall.

It falls differently every time.

It falls for the first time every time.

I said to Nanu that, when she turns nine, she'll see that there's no standard way to play the drone.

You come to it new every time.

The instrument is your closest friend but you discover it as if for the first time every time.

Singers and percussion players in Indian classical music approach the notes and beats as if they were not already there waiting for them.

These musicians have to coax and ask.

They build castles out of sand and fortresses out of snow every time.

They, therefore, never destroy. (Sound cannot be destroyed. Sound can only be reflected, refracted, or absorbed in its travel, its spreading out, its distribution.)

They're constantly building.

It just so happens that their materials are imaginary.

Sounds and moods and space evaporate into thin air the moment you let them be.

They're like snowflakes that melt one second after you catch them.

Indian classical music likes the drone, because it doesn't like to build patterns quickly.

Once you begin a pattern, you're stuck with it.

Once you see a pattern, it's hard not to see it.

It's hard to see anything else.

And once you build up speed, it's hard to not enjoy that acceleration.

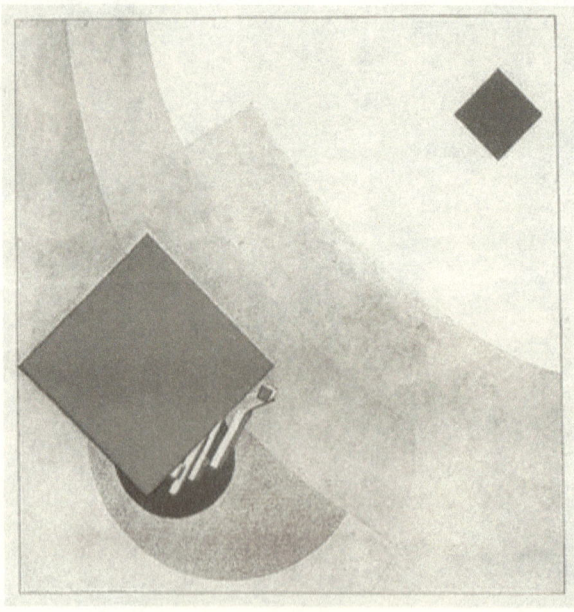

I asked Nanu if she was nervous about being one of the few drone players in her tradition.

Nanu said yes.

She said it's not called a drone: it's a sarangi.

She said that sometimes as you get older you forget things from your younger days.

At eight, she said, she still knew that rhythm is "expansion over time."

Rhythm is structured like a memory.

Even when you're in it, you're in and out of it.

Rhythm is like playing pretend.

Somewhere in you, you're aware that it's all play-pretend-imagine, but who's to say it's not more real than real?

Nanu said that sarangi rhythm doesn't come from you.

It comes out of you.

It's called out of you.

It comes from another place.

It comes from outside of consciousness.

Nanu said that when you really get into the music, you realize that you're the imaginary part of a complex expression.

You get deep in a rhythm.

They call it being in "the pocket."

You're under the rhythm's control.

You're under the influence — you're outside (you've escaped, you've been freed from) the boundaries of consciousness.

You've caught a glimpse of the beauty beyond being: a higher state of being.

It's like time is all on one axis, space is expanding through another axis, and you're untethered on an imaginary third axis.

"Music is never about exploring yourself," Nanu said.

"Music is all about getting out of yourself."

"The World will be Open," Nanu said, "because our Circle is Closed."

You can't keep going on forever.

There is a real end to everything.

"The real end to everything happens," Nanu said, "as soon as I start giving the world more than it can handle."

"The real end starts happening when you forget that you're supposed to be playing."

You've started playing and pretending so deeply, you've given away more than you ever had.

When snow falls, and falls, and falls, it gets weighed down on itself.

When snow falls, there's no sound.

But when you start getting out there and playing, it's like a chorus of loud crunching clouds.

Sounds reflecting everywhere softly.

"Sounds being absorbed everywhere, softly," Nanu

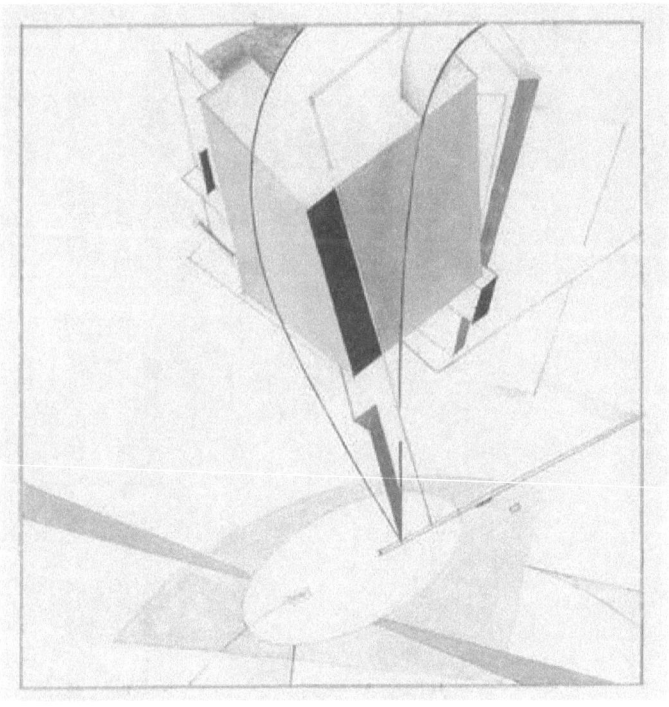

said.

"Don't you know that soft music gets loud at the end?"
Nanu said.

Chapter Six

With Open Arms (Nanu)

". . . I am approaching the end of my Romance . . ."

Nanu was the youngest of all my objects of study.

Eight years old.

She was a child of early spring, late winter.

Not wild like her mother (Lina).

Not stressed out like me (René).

Nanu was calm.

She was the mood of calm.

She was the experience of calm.

Calm like an ordinary Thursday evening.

Nanu liked to see the sun going down.

Thick golden layers of light would settle on the horizon.

As if light were laying itself flat.

Gray clouds would look down at themselves and see pink hues brightening them for a moment of evening time.

And what Nanu liked the most was seeing the tall, tall, leafless trees of winter swaying in the winds.

Tallness was tallness.

Leafless was leafless.

Trees were being trees all day long.

Winter could only be winter.

Swaying was swaying.

The wind was the wind.

Nanu knew all this — and nothing more — every evening.

(She translated *Nocturne* as *Evening* instead of *Night*.)

The evening was not an echo of her most intimate thoughts and emotions.

The evening was the evening.

Large birds woke up to hunt.

Other birds and animals hid and went to sleep in their homes, or wherever they found themselves safe.

Some people believe that a seed is planted early in the mornings at dawn; the rest of the day, they say, is simply the unfolding of (the) fate (of the seed).

These people believe fate to be uncompromising.

Fate will have its fulfillment, no matter what.

Such is the jealousy and invisible power of fate.

Nanu did not believe this.

She did not believe that every day was a story, with a beginning, middle, and end.

She did not believe that everything had a plot.

She did not believe that almost everything ends in tragedy, wherein we lose the one thing that meant something to us.

She did not believe that everything else ends in comedy, wherein what was lost was not worth holding on to to begin with.

Our time is not like a page in young adult novels, wherein every sentence tries to teach you something or warn you about something or advance the plot towards a direct confrontation of good versus evil or freedom versus fate.

Nanu believed that our time is like music.

"Where words end, music begins."

It is impossible to put music into words.

There are feelings for which words cannot be found.

And, yes, those feelings, nevertheless, arise in the heart and cry out for expression.

For that, we have oohs and aahs and all kinds of musical tones that call for attention.

Music is a language that takes you back to your past.

Music takes you through your memories without the feeling of wanting to start your life over again.

You can be tired, and music will give you a psychic or

spiritual energy.

Music gives you time to pause and weigh things.

Nanu really disliked music videos of the past that tried to demonstrate a plot to the songs.

She did not like opera or ballet.

She did not like plays or poems.

She liked the music videos of people just dancing, merely dancing, simply dancing, dancing dancing.

Time passing.

Music playing.

A woman dancing.

A robot dancing.

Why do we hesitate to dance all that we're thinking and feeling?

Perhaps we only think new thoughts and feel new feelings — perhaps we only think all the thoughts and feel all the feelings — the more we imagine.

Nanu liked to learn on her own.

She did not like schools or followings.

Isn't most of our education learning how to sit still, in any case?

Does a human being need to learn how to be thoughtful?

Does a living thing need help developing her voice?

Nanu liked to look at things, be there with them, in a way that does not try to understand everything about them.

Does that sound boring?

Or does that sound pretty lovely?

There were times when Nanu was looking out at all of the Earth — all of it, trees, people, animals, the games we play, the baths we take in the sea, our dances, our skating on the ice, our skies, rooftops, clouds, fogs, walkways, flowers, roads, cycles, motorcycles, necklaces, our hair, our jewelry, our hands, our boats and waterways, our holding hands, fish, cats, birds, tall grasses in the water, our cameras, films, videos, fruits, vegetables, kites, shorts, shoes, shirts, jerseys, uphill walks, jogging, running, driving, temples, carousels, amusement parks, laws, our quiet winds, cold winds, card games, our

togetherness and play, our balloons, billboards, advertisements, brooks, mountains, soccer games in the street, in the dust and dirt, our rainy days, our teachers, guides, friends, our salutations, our expansiveness, and uncontained desire — and she saw everything happening in this huge, empty, enclosed space.

The emptiness is significant.

Emptiness is what gives sound reverberation.

Sound waves go out in every direction, reflect off surfaces, diminish and delay (echo).

We are the surfaces.

We are everywhere.

We are alone in the emptiness.

Separate.

Like a solo string instrument.

Everything else is out there on its own.

The atmosphere is radiant.

Nanu was real like that.

The realist of all real things were the empty things.

Imagination.

Me.

You.

Memory.

The future.

The arrow of time.

Hunger.

Names.

What else?

Colors?

Laughter?

Gravity?

Sleep?

Voices over the telephone frequencies?

All of inner life?

Closed Circle Open World.

Nanu did not resist.

She said, "Yes."

She moved forward as if she saw hopscotch tiles on the ground, and a hula hoop around her waist.

Yes.

Nanu did not believe that artwork was the highest achievement of our beliefs.

She did not believe that a book would (or could) address the problems of our world.

After Thursday evening comes Friday morning.

Nanu was eight years old, remember.

What does a child of eight know that the rest of us have forgotten?

Time changes.

Times change.

Snow is wonderful.

Every creature on Earth likes to laugh.

Every creature has questions.

Everyone misses someone.

Everyone has love to give.

Some people, when they want to say goodbye, blow kisses.

Some fold their hands and bow their heads.

Some look right into your eyes, then blow kisses, then touch their heart, and point to the stars in the sky.

They're saying, "I'll be as close to you always as the stars."

The stars are not that far away.

There is no neutral place.

Truth is not neutral.

Truth appears and comes to — visits, takes by the hand — those who have an active imagination.

Imagination is literally seeing, sensing, hearing, holding, getting a mouthful of something real in the world that hits you like the key of F♯ minor at 81 BPM.

You know when music pulls you into the world? Makes you dance? Especially sometimes when it has low energy like that? Like, the music is asking you to move with it? And won't take *no* for an answer? Like, a deep, innocent seduction? And you didn't know you could be so immersed, so light, so free?

Dance is an art like no other.

Dance is like skating on ice.

Dance is as soundless as all the thoughts in our mind.

"The world is what you make of it."

Why do bad things happen to good people? You know when you see a rock, and you kick at it? You think the rock doesn't feel. Sometimes you want the rock not to feel. Sometimes you want the rock to feel as bad as you're feeling. Sometimes you just don't stop and think. Sometimes you don't stop, think, feel, and imagine. Sometimes you don't stop and ask. Sometimes you don't think that the rock likes you. Sometimes you think that no one would be able to like you. Sometimes you like being bad and mean. That's why sometimes we kick rocks. That's why bad things happen to good people. There are no two kinds of people. Everyone has an emptiness inside. Even rocks. Why do bad things happen to rocks? We don't think the rock has life?

The imagination is the extension of life.

Expansion of life.

Enlargement of life.

Elevation of life.

The stretching out.

The addition of beats.

Thickening of a melody.

You can believe whatever you want to believe.

Ask the rock, "Are you alive?"

Your question brings the rock to life.

Questions bring the world to life.

That empty feeling can be a sign of life.

That empty feeling is *the* sign that *still* there is life.

Still *there* is life.

Still there *is* life.

Still life is still life.

There is the drone, and there is the dance.

When you're eight, you feel that.

You know your imagination keeps everything alive.

When everything is still alive, you hear the drone music of the largest rock of all: the Earth just rocking and rolling along, circling, revolving, with the beat of a kick like an empty drum, like a heart.

When you're still alive, you can hear the sky cry, the snow cry, the wind cry, the leaves cry, the stones cry, the rivers cry, the winter cry, and you're glad for the emptiness that reverberates all these sounds.

All these cries are very far away.

Most of them don't even reach you.

Maybe as an echo in your heart, maybe.

At eight, the whole world is off in its corner, everyone working in their own separate spaces.

The world is not one.

The world is open.

Everything takes time.

A lot of time.

Take your time.

The future is not just an extension of the past.

Sometimes something happens out of the blue that changes what we thought was possible.

There's no explanation for what happened in the past.

You can only understand miracles backwards, once they've already happened, even though they were impossible just a minute ago.

There is nothing in Nature or The Skies telling us what to do.

When you're eight, you know that you are alone, and responsible for your fate.

You don't wait for things to happen to you.

When's the last time something really stopped you in your tracks?

Was it something you could measure? Or was it something new against which you had to recalculate everything?

The beginnings of drone music begin unmeasured.

The secret of playing the sarangi drone is that you have a melody with words in your head.

But you never sing the lyrics.

You keep them somewhere in between sound and silence.

This makes the instrument nothing less than haunting.

You hear only the rhythm of the drone that is produced neither by the musician, the bow, the string, the playing, but purely by the reverberations in empty space.

At eight, you hear only what speaks to you.

You start listening to the sounds of language more than the language.

In one note, you can hear every shape, sound, and color.

What if you were trying to fill the whole world with one note, and you looked up and saw someone who heard what you were trying to say?

And you could see that the key you've chosen to play in has stopped her in her tracks?

Wouldn't you want something like that?

Wouldn't that feel like Closed Circle?

Wouldn't that feel like Open World?

What will you do this time around?

The End

Acknowledgments

Thank you to everyone who made this book possible.

I dedicate this book to young people everywhere who want to change something about their lives.

Nothing is impossible.

Everything is a matter of belief.

If you desire to change something about your life — your fate or future — and are feeling scared about trying, *there's a belief behind that feeling* of fear (or hopelessness). Maybe you're afraid to speak up. Maybe you're afraid that no one will listen to you. Maybe you're scared that if you fail, you'll experience terrible embarrassment or disgrace. Maybe you've been told too often by too many people that you have no right to determine your future. Maybe there's even a lot of evidence that all your fears are warranted.

I understand these feelings.

We all understand. We may not admit it, but we all have them. We're all scared in these exact same ways.

But it is possible to change something about your life.

It is possible to take a risk, challenge yourself (believe in yourself), and go through the hardships and failures that come your way.

It won't be easy. But it won't be as hard as you think.

"What is the goal of life? Are we to just be what we are, and nothing more? What are we here for? . . . We are here to make ourselves free. All of nature is crying through all atoms for one thing: its perfect freedom." It's a struggle. It's not impossible.

Impossible and possible are not opposites.

Impossible is in the realm of the possible.

If you believe it's possible, if you get rid of the limiting — usually irrational — beliefs that define change to be impossible, then, change in your life is *surely* possible.

Think about it.

Talk about it.

"If we could get rid of the belief in our limitations, it would be possible for us to do everything just now. It is only a question of time."

You'll be rewarded when you prove to someone else — just like you — that change is possible. You'll feel like you were able to take away someone else's very real pain. You'll be able to show her what confidence looks like, and you'll ask her what it is she desires to change about her life. You'll be able to tell her that she has every right to speak up about her pains, her dissatisfactions, and her desires.

Illustrations in this book are by Aleksandra Ekster (1882 – 1949), Robert Falk (1886 – 1958), Natalia Goncharova (1881 – 1962), Ivan Kliun (1873 – 1943), El Lissitzky (1890 – 1941), Kazimir Malevich (1879 – 1935), Lyubov Popova (1889 – 1924), and Olga Rozanova (1886 – 1918).

Cover Image by Aleksandra Ekster, "Costume Design for Aelita," 1924.

About the Author

Shyam R. Gohel (b. April 1, 1982) is working on a new book for young adults (ages 12 – 15) on a topic older than "change your fate," namely, the topic of hurt feelings, lost relationships, and the grief that follows; the book will be in the oldest literary genre of despair-rage-revenge and questions of justice.

Books by Shyam include: Rana Spring Summer Fall, Asha Deep in My Heart Someday, Samira Is Wind (forthcoming), Mena 9 Years Old in Therapy (for ages 8 – 10), Nikhil the Noir Detective (ages 8 – 10), Be Present You're a Present (ages 5 – 9), 1 2 3 4 Let's Be Mindful (ages 3 – 7), Laugh Before You Sleep (ages 3 – 7), Why Do I Love? Why Do I Get Upset? (ages 3 – 7), There's a Flower in Your Heart (ages 3 – 7), and more.